Grand Theft

Crime Solver's Detective Agency – book 2

Victoria Schwimley

First printing

Characters in this book are fictitious, with the exception of the main characters, which may bear a slight resemblance to real persons. Any resemblance to other characters is purely coincidental.

ISBN-13: 978-0692483701
ISBN-10: 0692483705

Published by

PUBLISHING

This book is dedicated to all my grandchildren, whose love, enthusiasm for life and overall quirkiness give me hours of enjoyment and endless storylines

Chapter One

I was just coming off Christmas break, and dreading my return to school, when the best case of my career came my way. Mrs. Thornton's garage was broken into and her 1977 Mustang was stolen from it—right in broad daylight! She's my neighbor, so I heard about the case first hand.

Well, needless to say, the neighborhood was in a ruckus. Everywhere I turned, I heard shouts of, "It's not safe in our own neighborhood!" or, "What is happening to the neighborhood!" or, "I'm moving back to the Midwest where it's safe."

My head nearly spun with all the cries for help. "I can do this one," I said to my mother on the third day after the robbery. She was tidying up the playroom and I kept running in front of her, trying to catch her attention. I slapped a closed fist into my palm. "It's exactly what I've been looking for!"

She shook her head firmly and put on her serious—no room for negotiation—mother's face. "This isn't someone's lunch money stolen, or misplaced dogs." She cupped my chin in her hand and looked me straight in the eye. "This is too big for you to handle. Let the police do their work." She raised her eyebrows. "Do you understand me?"

I nodded. She let go of my chin and I stalked off to my bedroom to pout. I threw myself on the bed and pursed my lips. How could I stay out of something so big?

My phone rang. With barely any enthusiasm, I answered, "Crime Solvers. Do you have a crime for me to solve?"

"Hi, Karrine," came my little cousin's perky voice. She lives in Sacramento with her mother, my aunt. My grandparents live there, too. She had spent the summer with me and we solved some awesome crimes together. She was determined to start her own agency in Sacramento. I told her she could call any time if she needed some advice. I guess she needed some.

"Oh, hey, Jayden."

"What's the matter?" she asked. "You sound so glum."

I sighed, and rolled over. I plucked at a stray thread on my bedspread and winced when it pulled a whole string free. I tried patting it back in, but it wouldn't stay. I patted it down, pretended it stayed, and rolled the other way. "I've got the biggest case of my career." I told her about the break-in.

"That's great! I wish I was there to help you. All I got is a dumb missing grade book."

"It wouldn't matter anyway," I said. "Mother won't let me take the case."

"Why not!"

I sighed again. "She thinks it's dangerous."

"Well, maybe it is—a little," Jayden said.

"Not for an experienced detective like me," I said.

"I guess you're right," Jayden said. "Is this a bad time to ask for help?"

"Not at all," I said. "It will take my mind off my case that I can't work. What's up?"

"Someone stole my teacher's test book and now she's going to give a test twice as hard, unless I manage to find that test book. I'm sunk. It's in math, and I suck at math!"

I thought for a minute, tapped the phone with my thumb, causing it to make a screeching sound. "Who are your suspects?"

"So far, I only have two—Jacob Martindale and Mark Hesper."

I sat up, swung my legs over the edge of the bed and wandered over to my desk, where I picked up a pen. Poised and ready to write, I said, "Tell me about them."

"Jacob is new. He's my number one suspect," she said.

"What puts him at the top of your list?"

"Well…for one, he's new so no one knows anything about him."

"Go on," I urged. I needed more than that.

"He never raises his hand to answer a problem, so I figured he's dumb at math and needs the test answers to pass."

I nodded. "Good point, but there could be another reason for that." I hoped I didn't bring her down with my point.

"True," she said, not seeming at all shaken. "He also keeps to himself and refuses to answer any of my questions."

"Aha!" I said. "Sounds as if he's hiding something."

"That's what I thought," Jayden said. I could hear the pride in her voice.

"What about this Mark guy?"

Jayden paused. "The only thing I got on him was the fact he was seen in the hallway after school."

"Interesting," I said. "What did he give for a reason?"

"He said the football coach sent him to get some balls from the gym."

"Likely story," I said. "Did the coach confirm it?"

"Gee," Jayden said. "I haven't questioned the coach."

"Do that next," I said. "And see if you can find out where this Jacob kid came from. And see if there was any trouble reported involving him at his last school."

"Thanks, Karrine! I'll get right on that."

We said goodbye, and I slumped back into my gloom. Helping Jayden had only made me anxious for a new case.

"Karrine, supper," I heard my mother call from the dining room.

I rolled my eyes and shuffled my way to the kitchen. Mom's call to supper was really a call to set the table, so I went straight to the cupboard and took down plates. I let the door close a little too loudly and got what felt like a five-hour lecture about respecting my elders and doing what's expected of me. "I'm sorry, Mother," I said. "I'm just still a little sore about the big case."

She stopped stirring the spaghetti sauce and asked, "What big case?"

I shook my head as I placed eating utensils next to plates around the table. I stared opened-mouth. "The case...the really big one...grand theft auto," I said.

She nodded. "Oh...yeah...the case. Well, I'm sorry about that but, safety first you know." She set down the spoon and lifted the heavy pot from the stove and moved it to the table. Then she strained some pasta noodles and set the bowl on the table. "Call the boys," she said.

I went to the bottom of the stairs and shouted up, "Grub is on."

Thundering footsteps rushed past me as my brothers raced each other to the table. My step-father followed the boys, only he didn't run. I sat down at the table. My head hung low to my chin. "What's with you?" my step-father asked.

"Nothing," I grumbled.

My mother sat down with a heavy sigh. "Mrs. Thornton's car was stolen from her garage."

"And I want to work the case," I said, rushing in…hoping for an ally.

"And I think she's too young."

"Seems to me, it's a police matter," my step-father said.

I slumped back again. There went any hope of him being on my side.

"Besides," Mother said, "You don't even have a client."

I brightened. "So, if I had a client, could I?"

"Well you don't, so it's a moot point. Eat your dinner." She pointed at the plate I hadn't even touched. I was too depressed to eat.

After dinner, I went into the den and turned on the news. My mother walked in and saw me sitting there, staring at the television. She looked at what was on. "You're watching the news?"

I nodded, my eyes never leaving the screen. "Can't a girl be interested in what's going on in her own community?"

"She can," my mother said, "but since when are you a news buff?"

I took a quick glimpse at her and returned to staring at the television. "I'm getting older now," I said. "I'm turning thirteen next month. Don't you think it's time I acquainted myself with the goings on around me."

"Mm, hm," my mother said. "You're trying to see if you can find out any information about the stolen car."

I was astonished, insulted, ridiculed—and busted. "How'd you know?"

"It's my job," she said. She picked up the remote and flipped off the television. "You might have better luck if you Google the crime."

I jumped to my feet. "Of course!" I ran from the room, shouting my thanks over my shoulder. I skidded to a halt at the computer, sliding into the computer chair. At first, I got way too many hits when I Googled stolen car. Then when I added my street name to the search…BINGO, it was there. I searched the article, looking for any clues. Mother said I couldn't work the case, but she said nothing about following it on the internet. Buried deep in the newspaper, on about the sixth page, was a small blurb about the theft.

Apparently, the Las Vegas Crime Reporter didn't share my opinion about this being "the big case." I read that article four times and only learned that similar incidences were happening all over the city. Could this be a serial thief?

While I was online, I got an instant message from Jayden updating me on her own case. Our email conversation went like this:

Jayden: *Sorry about your big case.*

Me*: Thanks*

Jayden: *I tried calling Jacob's old school. They won't give me any information. The lady on the phone said it was none of my business.*

Me: *Well, keep trying. Maybe your mom will call them for you.*

Jayden: *Great idea. I'd better solve this case fast; our harder test is scheduled for Friday. That's only three days from now. Gotta run. Love you.*

Me: *Love you, too.*

I signed off and went to bed.

I was in a terrible gloom the next day. I was itching for a case, and at this point, I didn't care what it was. I wouldn't even mind if Mrs. Jackson got into some more trouble. She had pulled a really good prank on her husband, just to get his attention. But she wasn't clever enough to escape my sleuthing brain.

Pinky sent me a text saying Rusty was ready to go home. Last year, Mrs. Waverly, Rusty's owner, had summoned me to find her "stolen" dog. It turned out he was in Pinky's care and Mrs. Waverly had forgotten about asking Pinky to groom Rusty. I earned twenty dollars by finding him and returning him. Now, every time he went for a groom, Mrs. Waverly called saying someone kidnapped him and could she hire me to find him. I felt kind of guilty taking her money but, hey, if she can't keep track of her own dog, how is that my problem? Besides, it really helped Pinky.

When the school bell rang, dismissing school for the day, I sent my mom a text and told her I was headed over to Pinky's to take Rusty home. She responded by asking me to bring home milk with me. I sighed and said I would. Did any other private eye get asked by her mother to pick up things from the store on their way home from a case?

Pinky was glad to see me, as we had become good friends since the dog-napping case. Occasionally, she even had need of help around the dog-grooming salon, and she would pay me to wash dogs for her.

"That would be a great help," she said. "In fact, I'll give you an extra ten if you take Blue Bell, too."

My eyes lit up. Not only did I like Blue Bell, business was kind of slow at the minute, and I could use the money. "Sure," I said.

"I'll be right back," Pinky said, but halfway to the backroom she stopped and turned around. "Did you hear about the Stanley's Mustang?"

"You mean the Thornton's Mustang? Yeah, I heard about it."

Pinky's eyes flew open wide and she rushed back to the counter. "The Thornton's Mustang was stolen, too?"

My eyes went wide as well. "The Thorntons and the Stanleys!" It was starting to seem as if a crime wave was brewing. "Are there any leads?" I asked.

Pinky shrugged. "I was hoping you'd know. I thought you'd be all over this case."

My shoulders slumped into their now typical pose. I frowned. "My mother forbade me to touch it."

Pinky frowned from one side of her mouth. I was amazed she could do that. "I guess I can see her point."

"Well, I can't!" I screamed. "How am I supposed to be a top-notch crime solver if my mother won't let me work any cases beyond stolen lunch money?"

Pinky sprayed some perfume on Blue Bell, who sneezed and then growled. I sat up straight and waved the perfume fumes away. "It smells good," Pinky said, indignantly.

"Maybe a little bit," I said, "but you don't have to douse the dog with the entire bottle."

Pinky frowned. "What else do you have going?"

I slumped again. "Nothing."

She clipped on Blue Bell's leash and handed it to me. "I'll be right back."

Blue Bell clamped down on the leash and she and I began a game of tug-o-war. I was winning when Pinky reappeared with Rusty. She handed me his leash, too. We made our way to the door, Rusty nipping at Blue Bell all the way, and she looking at me with a pathetic *help me* look. "This is going to be interesting," I muttered.

I hopped on my bike and tied a leash to each handlebar. Rusty immediately began to run. Poor Blue

Bell's little legs worked with a frenzy to keep up. "Slow downnnnnnnnnn!" I screamed at Rusty. By this time, Rusty had spotted a puppy scampering under a fence. He increased his speed. I must have been going at least sixty miles per hour, judging from the way my hair blew out behind me. "Stop it right now, Rusty!" I screamed again. He didn't listen to me one bit, and now both dogs were chasing at high speed. I slammed on my brakes...big mistake; I flew over the handlebars and for the first time was grateful of my mother's insistence I wear a bicycle helmet. My head collided with the fence. I saw stars spin above my head. My knee was bleeding—nothing a little Band-Aid wouldn't help—and I felt like a fool.

Three people rushed over to me...yes, it's true some humans still care. Unlike the four-legged monsters who now sat barking at the fence they never had any chance of making it through. Rusty looked at my frowning face, whined, and licked my hand.

"Are you okay," someone asked.

I looked up into the face of the cutest boy in school. Jared Sinclair. I had never met Jared because I was too intimidated to talk to him, but here he was jumping to my rescue. He extended his hand down to me. His face wore the cutest, hugest, smile I'd ever seen.

My knees shook as he helped me stand. "Are you all right?"

I nodded. "That was a close one."

He looked down at Rusty and Blue Belle. "How are your dogs?"

I ruffled Rusty's head and gave Blue Belle a little stroke. "They're not mine. I'm just doing a favor for a friend and returning them home."

"Here," he said, "let me take one of them for you. My name's Jared."

"Yes, I know," I said, smiling at him.

"Don't we have English together?"

I nodded. "Science, too."

"That's what I thought. You're the smart girl who sits at the front of the class."

"I'm not that smart," I said, as if being smart were a bad thing.

He chuckled and I noticed he had the cutest dimples. Why hadn't I ever noticed them before?

We walked past the ice cream shop. Mr. Scoops was sweeping the sidewalk outside. He waved. "Good afternoon, Karrine," he called.

I waved back. "Hey, Mr. Scoops."

"I've got tables to clean. Busy lunch period today."

I held up Rusty's leash, pointed at Blue Belle and said, "Sorry, I'm taking these critters home for Pinky." My mouth suddenly filled with the taste of strawberry ice cream. "I could stop on the way back," I said.

He waved. "I'll save them for you."

We walked on and I explained my arrangement with Mr. Scoops. "I help him out in exchange for free ice cream."

"Sweet deal," Jared said.

We came to Rusty's house. "You wait here with Blue Belle. Mrs. Waverly doesn't do well with strangers." I started to walk toward the door, paused and then looked back at Jared. "Come to think of it, she doesn't do well with people she knows, either."

I shook my head and made my way up the driveway. I knocked on the door. From the other side, Mrs. Waverly said. "Who is it?"

"It's me, Mrs. Waverly, Karrine."

Her voice turned hard and lowered as if she were trying to sound like a man. "Karrine who?"

I shook my head, turning around to smile at Jared. I waved my finger in circles, indicating she was slightly cuckoo. He smiled back. "I've got Rusty for you."

She flung open the door and snatched him from my hands. "Thank goodness," she said. "I was just about to call the police." She looked at me and narrowed her eyes. "Young lady! Just who do you think you are stealing my Rusty?" She made kissy noises at him, puckering up and smacking her lips. "You poor darling." She slammed the door.

My shoulders dropped, I sighed, shook my head back and forth and knocked again.

"Who is it?" Mrs. Waverly said in a singsong voice.

I sighed again. "It's Karrine," I said.

"What's wrong with her?" Jared shouted to me.

"Nothing," I shouted back. "She's just trying to get out of paying."

Jared joined me on the doorstep and said, "Maybe she has that Alzheimer's thing. My grandpa has it. He can't remember a thing."

I frowned. "Gee, I hope not," I said, "I'd feel bad if she really does." I banged again.

"Who is it?" Mrs. Waverly said.

I grunted. Jared grinned at me. He said, "It's UPS. I have a package for you."

The door flung open wide and Mrs. Waverly stood on the porch, still holding Rusty. "Where?" she said, trying to look for the package. I held out my hand and tapped my palm. She sighed in defeat. "Oh, all right," she said.

She put Rusty on the ground, where he proceeded to growl at Jared. "Is that dog going to bite me?"

I put a hand out to Rusty. "Good boy," I said. He immediately sat and wagged his tail at me. When I first met Rusty, the entire community was afraid of him. He bit and barked, and chased anything that moved. With my patient teaching, he had become a much friendlier dog. "He'll be fine," I said.

Mrs. Waverly returned with her wallet and handed me ten dollars. I waved my fingers to indicate I needed more. I was collecting Pinky's fee, too. She started muttering something about a fixed income, which meant nothing to me. When she counted out the right amount of bills, I thanked her and waved, stooped to give Rusty a pat, and walked away. The door slammed behind me. I grinned at Jared.

Delivering Blue Belle was a piece of cake, and we even got milk and homemade chocolate chip cookies as a bonus.

"Is this what you do with your free time?"

"Naw," I said," just when business is slow. I usually spend my time solving mysteries." My frown appeared. "I'm just in between cases right now. There's a really big case going on right now, but my mother won't let me work it." I felt foolish the minute the confession left my mouth. I sounded like a whiny baby.

"What if you had a partner?"

I thought about this for a minute. I wondered how I'd feel with someone else sharing my adventure. "I've used my cousin Jayden before, but she went home."

Jared stopped and spread his arms out wide. "How about me?"

I stopped and looked at him. I could feel my eyes grow large with surprise. "You!"

"Sure. I don't see why not." He stood up straight, stuck out his chest and chin, grabbed the edge of his jacket, and stuck his elbow out like a clucking chicken. "I'd make a great detective."

I stared quietly at him. Crime Solvers was my agency. I didn't know how I'd feel about sharing the glory with Jared...even if he was the cutest boy in school.

I started walking again. Jared gave me a minute to think. We were coming up to Mr. Scoop's store and I hesitated before going in. I looked at Jared. He looked at me. "I usually work alone," I said.

"But this is a really big case, and you said your mother wouldn't let you work it."

I frowned. Jared was standing there with a really stupid grin on his face, showing me his beautiful, pearly-white teeth. He tipped his head sideways and stuck out his lower lip. He whined like a dog.

I stomped my foot on the ground. "That's not fair. You know how much I love dogs."

"Is that a yes?"

I thought back to the conversation with my mother. Had she actually said I couldn't do it? A smile came to my lips. No, she hadn't. What she said was it was too big for me to handle, but wasn't that just her opinion? Her warning to let the police handle it didn't mean a thing, as I had no intention of interfering with their investigation. I was just going to do one of my own. "All right," I said. "But don't get in my way."

He clapped his hands. "Where do we start?"

"At the scene of the crime."

We hurried back to my house to make our plan.

Chapter Two

My cell phone rang just as Jared and I were walking through the front doorway. I looked at the caller ID and saw the call was from Jayden. I looked over my shoulder at Jared. "It's my cousin. I have to take it. I'm helping her with a crime." I pushed the answer button and said into the phone, "Hey, Jayden." I indicated Jared should sit at the table while I went to the refrigerator and got out the milk. I poured us both a glass and then hoping against hope that Mother had baked that day, I closed my eyes and plunged my hand into the cookie jar, bringing back ooey, gooey, chocolate chip cookies. A huge grin broke out on both my and Jared's faces.

"Hey, Karrine," Jayden said. "Boy, do I need some help."

I flopped down on the chair next to Jared. He smiled at me with a mouthful of cookie. "Sorry," I mouthed. He shrugged, which I took to mean was okay with him.

"Shoot," I told Jayden. I took a pen and paper out of my backpack as I listened.

"I followed Jacob home after school today," she said.

"You what!" I exclaimed.

"Don't worry," she said, "I was extra careful not to be seen."

"What happened?" I said. My cousin had a lot more spunk than I gave her credit for.

"He lives way out of town. I thought we'd never get there. He must have taken about a million turns before we finally came to his house, and boy, what a house he has. He has like fifteen bedrooms and a gazillion—"

"Jayden," I said. I had to stop her or she might have gone on all night, and I really needed to get back to my own crime.

"What?" she said.

"The crime."

"What about it?"

"You were telling me about when you followed your suspect."

"Oh, yeah, that." She giggled. "Well, it was easy to hide once I got there. The house was ginormous!"

"Did you find anything?"

"Only that he has some kind of tree house in his back yard."

"Yeah!" I said. I'd always wanted a tree house, but it had never worked out for me. "What was in it?"

"I don't know yet. I couldn't get too close because I was afraid I'd get caught. I'm going to go back tomorrow while he's at football practice."

"What are you going to do?"

"I'm going to search the tree house."

"Okay," I said. "Let me know what you find. Any luck finding someone to call his old school?"

"Oh, yeah. My friend Sasha's older sister is going to do it. Sasha said she'd have a report ready for me at school tomorrow."

"Okay, then. Call me after you scope out the tree house. What about the football coach?"

"Not at school today so I couldn't talk to him."

"All right then. Try again tomorrow and call me."

"Okay. Bye, Karrine."

"Bye, kiddo," I said. I closed my phone. "My kid cousin," I said to Jared. He nodded. "She solves crimes, too." He nodded again. I stuffed another cookie into my mouth so I didn't feel so stupid. I stood up and put the cookie jar back. Jared followed me to my room.

My mother called to me as I passed her door. "Is that you, Karrine?" I rolled my eyes and shook my head. I'd been in the house twenty minutes and NOW she asks if it's me. "Yes, Mom," I said. "My friend, Jared, is with me."

That brought her to the doorway. "Hello," she said.

Jared moved his head slightly in what I supposed was a nod. "Hey," he said.

From the look Mother gave him, I'd guess he wasn't earning brownie points with her.

"Let's go," I said. I started to walk toward my room. "We're going to see what's going on in the Thornton case. Okay, Mother?"

Mother frowned. "Perhaps you should find a new hobby, Karrine. The community center is making model airplanes, and they're going to really fly. I'm taking the boys. Want to come?"

OMG! Did my mother actually just call my business a hobby? "Uh," I said. "I think we'll pass on the airplanes." I started off toward my room. "We're just going to get my computer and then we're heading out."

"Okay," Mother said. "If you're sure? I heard there's going to be a contest for the best airplane."

OH, YEAH, DEFINITELY, SURE! I smiled. "It's okay, Mom," I said. "You make one for me."

I grabbed my laptop very quickly, before Mother could insist I accompany her to the community center, and Jared and I headed back down the stairs at a cheetah's pace. I think I might have heard Mother call to me, but I couldn't be sure.

"Where are we headed?" Jared asked.

I glanced back at the house. "Anywhere but the community center," I said.

Jared shrugged. "I think it sounded kinda fun."

I narrowed my eyes. "Crime solving is a serious business. Do you want to play like a kid, or solve crimes?" He looked at the house and frowned. "Are you kidding me!" I screamed.

Jared grinned at me. "Naw. Let's go."

I started to walk down the driveway. "We'll start with interviewing Mrs. Thornton."

I knocked on her front door. She opened it rather quickly, an expectant look on her face. "Did you find my…" Her face fell to sadness when she saw I wasn't the police. Her shoulders slumped. "Oh, Karrine. I thought you were the police."

I put my hand on her arm and gave her a sympathetic look. "I'm so sorry about your car, Mrs. Thornton. I know how much you and Mr. Thornton loved it." It was true, too. They didn't even drive anymore on account of Mr. Thornton's eyesight is bad. And he won't let Mrs. Thornton drive it. He says she isn't careful enough and always forgets where she parked it. Whenever they had to go somewhere, their son or daughter would take them. Sometimes my mother would give Mrs. Thornton a ride to the grocery store.

Mrs. Thornton dabbed at a tear. "We were going to give it to our grandson, Timmy. He's graduating from high school this year and we thought it would be the perfect gift."

I'd heard the expression, "his jaw dropped" but never really knew it was true. Well, it is because Jared's jaw dropped beside me. I elbowed him.

"Ow," he cried. I elbowed him again.

Mrs. Thornton looked at Jared holding his side. "Is something wrong?"

"Nothing at all," Jared said between clenched teeth.

"We'd like to ask you some questions," I said.

Mrs. Thornton's eye flew open wide in surprise. "Of course. I forgot that you have that little crime business."

She ran off then and I could hear her rummaging through a drawer in the kitchen. I knew it was the kitchen because I had spent many a summer afternoon sipping lemonade with her. She was a very nice person and didn't deserve to have her car stolen.

She came back to the living room and declared, "Here it is!" She held a card in her hand and started reading from it, tracing the words with her finger. She had a huge smile on her face. "Crime Solver's Detective Agency. I just knew I'd have use of this someday. Are you going to solve the crime for me, Karrine?"

I sighed. How could I tell this sweet old woman, who had so much faith in me, that my mother wouldn't let me help her, the one and only time I could pay her back for all that lemonade I drank. I looked at Jared, who raised his eyebrows at me and shrugged his shoulders.

I looked at Mrs. Thornton, who stood there with her lower lip trembling, her eyes glistening with pleading tears. Then she did it, she gave me the puppy-dog head tilt and that's all that was needed. I smiled. "Of course I'll solve your crime for you."

Chapter Three

At school the next day, I started asking questions. Jared hung by me whenever he could, but he had some club he had to go to after school. "Don't do any sleuthing without me," he said.

"I won't. I told Pinky I'd help her in the salon after school."

"Okay," Jared said. "Let's put our heads together at lunch." He took off.

I wasn't very good at putting my head together with someone else. I usually work alone, if I haven't already told you that. Although, I had to admit, it was a lot easier solving mysteries when Jayden was around.

We met up at lunch and came up with a plan. I told Jared about the Stanley's car also being stolen. "Do they know each other?" he asked.

"Good question," I said. "I don't know, but we'll ask." I wrote the question down in my notebook. "We'll need to ask Mrs. Thornton some more questions."

Jared tilted his head and started to whine like a puppy. I hit him playfully with my notebook and giggled. "Stop that." He whined some more. I scooted farther down the bench. He whined some more. I scooted some more, until I had nowhere else to scoot. Then he stopped.

"We'll need to ask what color the cars were. Mrs. Thornton's was blue." I jotted down a note. "We'll have to ask the Stanleys what color theirs was."

Just then I heard sobbing coming from the corner of the cafeteria. I turned to look and saw Ms. Strawberry crying in the corner. Strawberry isn't really her name, but her hair always smells like strawberries because of the shampoo she uses, so everyone calls her that. It's been so long since anyone addressed her by her real name I don't even remember it. I asked her once if this bothered her, but she said she liked having a nickname. "It makes me feel accepted," she said.

"Come on," I said, not waiting to see if Jared would follow me.

There was already a crowd of kids surrounding her, but I elbowed my way through. "Excuse me," I said, "Karrine from Crime Solvers here. Is there a crime to solve?"

Ms. Strawberry's sobbing had died down to a sniffle by the time I made it to her. I whipped out a business card and handed it to her. She looked at the card and nodded. "Yes, Karrine, there is a crime. Someone stole my Mustang right out of the parking lot." She sniffed, sobbed again, only it was more like an agonizing wail. I had to cover my ears, as did several people around me.

I turned to Jared, who wasn't quite as pushy as I and was still only halfway to the center of the scene. I reached out, grabbed his hand, and pulled him the rest of the way through the crowd. My eyes danced with excitement. "It's a crime wave!"

Ms. Strawberry was back to the sniffle now. "Can you help?"

I puffed out my chest, nearly insulted at the notion of the word CAN. "Of course I can help! There hasn't been a crime yet I haven't solved."

Okay, forgive me my lack of modesty, but it really is true. I've solved every one of my crimes. Maybe some weren't actually crimes…a lost little something here or there, but I'd solved the mystery nonetheless.

I took a contract out of my backpack and looked at Jared. "Never start without a contract."

"You didn't have Mrs. Thornton sign one."

"Shh," I said. I leaned over and whispered, "That's on the house because I'm not really supposed to be working the crime, and she gives me lemonade all the time."

Jared pulled his eyebrows together the way some people do when they're thinking really hard. Then he said, "How is this any different?"

I rolled my eyes and shook my head. I was going to have to get rid of this tag-along conscience. I turned back to Ms. Strawberry and handed her the contract. She eagerly signed it and handed it back to me.

"Take us to the scene of the crime," I said.

Ms. Strawberry nodded and led the way. We walked past the teacher's lounge. I could see a bunch of teachers laughing and drinking coffee. This was interesting to me. I didn't know teachers knew how to laugh. I thought they all were so busy yelling at students, they didn't have time to be happy. This somehow made me feel a little less guilty.

We walked out a back door, which I didn't even know existed, and entered the forbidden STAFF parking lot. I had never seen this side of the building before. A huge gate that had to be opened with a card blocked the entrance to the parking lot. My mother always complained about this because she had to drive by it when she dropped me off at school. She said it would be a whole lot more convenient if she could drop me off here instead of fighting the traffic in front of the school. Now that I was standing in it, it didn't seem so special.

Ms. Strawberry walked three rows over, passing several really nice cars. I didn't know much about cars, but I know my mother said anyone who drives an Infiniti must be rich. I guess teachers make more money than I thought. I quickly did the math in my head. At the elementary level a teacher had about thirty-two kids in her class for six hours each day. That's a lot of bratty kids to look after every day, but when I thought about the junior high level, which I was, that was about 160 kids a day. Wow! That's a lot of bratty kids to put up with. Maybe teachers don't make enough.

She stopped in an empty parking spot. "This is it." She sniffled again. "This is where I left my baby this morning." She clutched a tissue to her chest and started crying again. "She misses me, I can feel it." Then she sobbed.

I shook my head. If she didn't stop crying all the time we'd never get this crime solved. I touched her arm to make her stop. "Ms. Strawberry, if you don't stop crying we'll never get anywhere in the investigation."

She nodded rapidly and wiped her eyes with her tissue. "Yes, of course. I'm sorry."

Suddenly I felt like the teacher. I began looking around.

"What are you doing?" Jared asked.

"I'm looking for anything out of the ordinary."

"Like what?" Jared asked.

"Something left behind that a teacher wouldn't normally leave." We both started looking. I had almost given up when I spotted something, "Aha!" I cried. I bent down and picked up a chewing gum wrapper. I held it up "Tutti-frutti bubble gum chewer." I turned to Ms. Strawberry and held it out to her. "Is this yours?"

"Of course it isn't mine," she said.

"Yes, but I know whose it might be." I pursed my lips together and stomped back toward the school building. Jared and Ms. Strawberry rushed behind me.

"Where are we going?" Jared asked.

I turned abruptly, a wild look to my face, eyes bulging, glistening with excitement. "Last year, Willie Sparks got in trouble for leaving Tutti-frutti bubble gum under his desk." I flapped my arms. I was excited. "The janitor found it when he was scraping off a piece from the floor under Willie's desk. He looked up and saw a whole bunch of wads of gum. Willie got suspended for a week."

"What does that have to do with this?" Jared asked.

"Karrine thinks Willie might have dropped this by my car." Ms. Strawberry had a smile on her face. "Good thinking," she said.

I beamed a huge smile. It felt great to have a teacher think something I did was good. "If we hurry maybe we can catch him before the lunch bell rings." It rang just then. "Oh, no!" I exclaimed. I started running. Ms. Strawberry and Jared ran, too. Willie had English with me, and that's where I was headed now.

I grabbed Willie's arm just as he was about to enter the classroom.

"Hey! What're you doing?" He tried to shake my hand loose, but I held on firmly. "Let go," he said.

I poked him in the nose with the gum wrapper. "Not until you explain this."

His eyes opened wide as he looked past me to Ms. Strawberry. "I…I…I…can explain that," he said.

I tapped my foot, shook the paper under his nose. "Start explaining."

He looked back and forth between Ms. Strawberry and me. "Some guy gave me twenty dollars to let him into the teacher's parking lot."

"For what?" I asked. My eyes narrowed and I pursed my lips at him.

"I don't know. I didn't ask."

Ms. Strawberry asked, "Why would you do that, Willie? You know students aren't allowed in the teacher's parking lot."

"Oh, no! He wasn't a student. He was an older guy— at least high school."

"You have to have a key card to get in there," Ms. Strawberry said.

I grabbed Willie's shirtfront. I can be pretty intimidating when I want. "Where'd you get the keycard?"

Willie looked down at the ground. Then he reached in his back pocket and pulled out a keycard. He handed it over to Ms. Strawberry. "I was going to slip it back in your desk next period."

Ms. Strawberry's mouth opened and closed. "You took this from my purse?"

"Yes, Ma'am," Willie said. "I'm sorry, if that helps."

She grabbed hold of his arm. "We're going to explain this to the principal."

She started to walk away with Willie. I called after her. "Wait." She stopped and I walked the few steps to where they now stood. "I have to ask Willie some questions first."

"Of course. I'm sorry," she said.

I'm about three inches taller than Willie, which is a good advantage when trying to interview a suspect. I took out my notebook and got ready to write. "What did this guy look like?"

"I don't know. He looked like lots of dudes."

I rolled my eyes. I could see I was going to have to get specific with this suspect. "What color was his hair?"

Willie shrugged. "Brown, I guess."

"You guess?"

"No, I'm sure. It was brown."

"How long," I said.

He shrugged again. "About like mine."

I frowned and looked hard at Willie. His hair was about to his chin. I held my hand to my chin. "About here?"

"Yeah, I guess." I frowned. "Okay, yes, to his chin."

"How tall?"

"Geez, Karrine. I don't carry a tape measure with me."

"Estimate," I said. "You can do that, can't you?"

He looked over at Ms. Strawberry. "About like her," he said.

Ms. Strawberry said, "I'm 64 inches tall."

"Young or old," I asked Willie.

"Young," he said.

I wrote on my notebook. *High school age.* "Where did you meet him?"

"At the pizza house. I was there with my family last week and when I was playing video games he came up and asked me if I'd like to make twenty bucks. I said I would, and he asked if I could get hold of a gate card to the teacher's parking lot. I told him I thought I could, and he said to meet him at the gate right after the start of school." He looked at Ms. Strawberry. "I know the teachers all get together for coffee in the lounge in the morning, so I waited for you to go in there. Then I snuck into your classroom and picked the lock to your desk. Those things aren't very secure, you know. You shouldn't leave your purse in there."

"Apparently," Ms. Strawberry said, her cheeks turning red.

"Okay," I said. "You can take him away," I told Ms. Strawberry.

"You need to go to class," Ms. Strawberry told Jared and me.

I nodded. I went to class but couldn't concentrate. All I kept thinking about was this guy. I closed my eyes, trying to envision anyone I know who might fit that description. Nobody came to mind.

"Karrine."

I looked up to see Mr. Stansbury standing over my desk. "Are you in this class today or what?"

I cringed. "Not really," I said. "I have this really terrific mystery I'm trying to solve and—"

"Solve your mysteries on your own time," he said. He walked away.

I slunk down in my seat as all the kids started to giggle.

As soon as class was over, I dashed out of there.

"Don't forget your homework," Mr. Stansbury said. I waved him off. Of course I'd do my homework.

Jared was waiting for me in front of the school. "Come on," I said.

"To the Pizza House?"

"You bet."

"What about questioning Mrs. Thornton?"

"This is a bigger lead."

"What about your club?"

"This is way more exciting than poetry. What about Pinky?"

"She'll understand," I said. "She knows how I am when I'm on a big case."

We both rode our bikes that day, so we hopped on and pedaled off. The Pizza House was only ten blocks from the school, so we got there quick.

The place was practically empty, but I knew that would change as soon as the school crowd caught up to us. I rushed up to the counter. A pimply-faced boy with red hair the color of carrots was standing there. "What do you want?" he asked.

"Shouldn't you say, 'How may I help you'?"

"I'm sixteen," he said. "I don't talk like that."

"Maybe you should," I said. "If more kids spoke correctly, we might have a better reputation."

He narrowed his eyes in an evil glare. "I don't care about nobody's reputation. Do you want pizza or not?"

"Not," I said.

"Then move over and let someone who does order. Next," he said.

"Wait. I have some questions."

"Unless it has to do with pizza, get out of here. Next," he called again.

Jared tapped me on the shoulder. "I'm kind of hungry. Maybe we could ask the questions while we order the pizza."

I sighed. "Okay." I looked at the pimply-faced boy. "I'd like a pepperoni pizza, and I'd also like to know if a tall kid from high school with brown hair and about 64 inches was in here today."

The kid stared at me as if I were from Mars. He shook his head. "How should I know? I'm stuck here all day at this stupid counter, waiting for you stupid kids to come in and order your stupid pizzas. I don't know what color anybody's hair is, or how tall they are for that matter. What kind of crust do you want?"

Jared leaned over my shoulder. "Super thin so there aren't too many carbs," he said.

The guy looked at Jared. "Carbs! Are you some kind of sissy? Pfft," he scoffed. He turned around and shouted to someone in the kitchen. "Hey, guys, Sissy guy out here is worried about carbs."

They all laughed. Jared's lip started to tremble. I jabbed him in the ribs to take his mind off it. To the kid, I said, "It's because of me. I'm trying to shed a few pounds." I frowned at Jared. He owed me one.

The kid looked me up and down from head to toe. "All right then. I guess you could shed a couple of pounds."

"Hey!" I exclaimed.

Jared nudged me. "The questions, Karrine."

"Oh, yeah. Give us some water glasses, too. And while you're at it, can you tell me if anyone's been in here talking about Mustangs lately?"

"I don't know," pimply face said. "I hate cars." He nodded toward the dining room. "Ask Jimmy. Jimmy knows all about cars."

"Thanks," I said. I started to walk away. "You didn't pay for your pizza," he said.

"Jared's going to pay."

"Hey!" Jared said.

"You wanted it," I said, waving back over my shoulder.

Jared sighed as I walked across the room to find Jimmy.

He wasn't hard to find, since there was only one person wearing a Pizza House uniform. I walked up to him. He had his back turned and was wiping down a table. "Are you Jimmy?"

The guy spun around. "Yeah. What you want."

I shook my head at him. "Repeat after me…I'm Jimmy. How may I help you?"

He smiled. "You're Jimmy, too. But you're a girl."

Perhaps I would be better suited to give free grammar lessons. It probably paid better than crime solving. I sighed. "No, I'm Karrine. You may help me by answering some questions about a guy who likes Mustangs."

He grinned hugely. "What year?"

"1977, or there about." I wasn't sure how old Ms. Strawberry's was, but I knew the Thornton's was a 77 and the Stanley's was just about as old.

"Ask me anything," he said, still grinning.

"Was—"

"The first Mustang was produced in 1965. It was—"

"I don't care about the car," I said. "I want to know about a guy who wants to steal them."

His grin faded. I felt bad. "Perhaps you can tell me about the car later, but first there's a string of car thefts going on and our suspect seems only to be interested in Mustangs. Older models," I added.

"Wow!" he said. He sat down with the rag and spray bottle still in his hand. His eyes looked dazed.

"Are you okay?" I asked. He slowly looked up at me.

"I didn't know," he said.

"Know what?" I asked. My heartbeat started thudding in my chest.

Jared came back with the pizza, but I was too nervous now to eat. It didn't seem to affect Jared, though, as he stuffed a second piece into his mouth.

"I didn't know he was going to steal them," Jimmy said.

"You know who I'm asking about?" I was more than excited. I tapped Jared's arm. "We have a lead."

"Ow," Jared said. His mouth was full of pizza, so it came out somewhat muffled, like, "www."

I wrote in my notebook. "When was he in here?" I asked Jimmy.

Jimmy's mouth did a sort of dance as he tried to speak. "I swear I didn't know. He just came up to me and said he'd heard I was into Mustangs. He said he was interested in buying one and asked if I knew who in the area had one."

"And you just gave him peoples' names and addresses."

Jimmy's mouth fell open and a hurt look flashed across his face. "Of course not!" Then he frowned. "I just gave him the names. If he figured out where they lived he did that himself."

I frowned and tipped my head sideways at him. "It's not that hard to figure out."

"Well…" he said. He sighed. "I have to get back to work."

He got up to walk away. I shouted after him. "Do you know where I can find him?"

He shook his head but didn't turn around.

"How about a name?"

He shook his head again. Then he stopped. He came back to me. "I don't know his name, but he had a friend with him, and he called his friend Stinker."

I couldn't help it, I started laughing. "Stinker! Are you sure?"

Then Jimmy grinned. "Yeah, I'm sure. The dude let out a good one at least five times while he was here." Jimmy shook his head. "The dude needs to do something about his diet." He walked away laughing.

Jared was still stuffing pizza into his mouth, but paused to say, "Do you really think his name is Stinker?"

I laughed even harder. "I'm sure it's not." I grabbed a slice before Jared could eat it all. When I swallowed, I said, "Let's recap."

My phone rang. I took it out of my pocket and looked at caller ID. "It's Jayden."

Jared got up to get some more water. "Me too," I hollered after him. He waved me off.

"Hey, cuz. What's up?"

"I'm so glad you picked up," Jayden said. She was out of breath.

"Whoa," I said. "Is everything okay?"

"No!" Jayden said.

"What happened?"

Jayden took some deep breaths and then she could talk a little better. "It's Jacy! She tagged along with me today when I went to Jacob's house, and now she's trapped in there!"

I widened my eyes, and then I gasped. "Oh, no! How did that happen?" Jacy is Jayden's little sister, also my cousin, in case you didn't figure that out. She's only six and gets in lots of trouble.

"I told her not to follow me, but she wouldn't leave me alone. I had no choice but to let her come. When I told her no, she said she was going to tell my mother that I was sneaking over to a boy's house."

"That dirty rat," I said.

"That's what I said," Jayden said.

Jared set down a soda in front of me. I gave him thumbs up. Then I wrote on a napkin that he should ask around and see if he could find out any more information about Stinker. I chuckled, just thinking about his name.

"Karrine! Are you listening to me?"

I snapped my attention back to Jayden. "I'm sorry. So tell me how she got trapped."

"Well, it all happened so fast. We waited outside the gate to his house for him to go inside. Then we climbed over. Jacy had a hard time and got stuck at the top, but I managed to get her down. There are bushes everywhere, so it was easy to hide. We made our way along the fence, being sure to stay beside the bushes. We made it all the way to the garage without getting caught."

I gasped. "And then what?"

"Jacy opened the door and an alarm started ringing."

"Oh, no!"

"Oh, no, is right. Two great-big dogs came out of nowhere!"

"Did you run?"

"I did. I shouted 'run for it', and I thought Jacy was right behind me, but when I turned back to look at her, a man had her by the arm and was leading her to the house.

It was awful. She was calling my name, but I didn't know what to do."

"Oh, no!" I said again, for lack of something clever to say. "Where are you now?"

"I'm still here. I climbed up into a tree so the dogs wouldn't get me, but they're lying on the ground at the bottom of the tree. They won't let me down. I don't know what to do."

It was time to put on my thinking cap. Only, I didn't know what to do either. I tried to think what I might do if I were there. "Do you have anything you could give the dogs?"

"Like what?"

"I don't know, a ball, something leftover from your lunch."

"I don't carry balls with me, and I had hot lunch today."

That was a disappointment. Okay, think Karrine. "Anything in your backpack they might like to play with?"

"Let me check."

I heard some rustling and assumed she was looking through her backpack. I took a moment to think about my own case. Where might I find a guy named Stinker? Obviously, that wasn't his real name. And what would they want with all those Mustangs? A person could only drive one car at a time, right?

"Oh, no!" Jayden exclaimed.

"What!"

"My mother is coming."

"Oh, no!" I said back.

"What should I do?"

I tried to think what I would do if it were my mother. "Play it cool," I said. "Take charge of the situation. Let them know you're the boss."

"Jayden, get down from there, right now," I heard my Aunt say.

"Too late," I whispered, but Jayden didn't let me down.

From the other end, I heard. "Hey, Mom. What are you doing here?"

The call disconnected. I would have to check in with Jayden later.

When Jared returned to the table, he was bouncing with excitement. He flopped down on the bench across from me, grinning wider than anyone I've ever seen anyone grin before. "Guess what I found out?"

I grinned back. "What?"

A twinkle came to his eyes. "I don't know if I want to tell you."

"Jared! This is my case, remember?"

"Our case," he said.

I rolled my eyes. "My detective agency. Now spill."

He rolled his eyes upward, like he was thinking hard. "Well, okay. Nobody seems to know our suspect, but everyone knows Stinker, for obvious reasons."

"That's awesome! What did you learn about him?"

"His real name is Horace Sprinkles." Jared started laughing. I laughed too.

"Poor guy can't win in the name department, can he?" I said.

Jared was chuckling. "Stinker Sprinkles. Can you believe that?" He was laughing hysterically. So hard in fact that he started coughing. Between bouts of laughter, he said, "Nobody could say his name with a straight face."

I pointed at him. "Including you." And then I laughed again. I took a deep breath. "Okay, let's get serious."

Jared was gasping, so I gave him a few seconds. "Okay, I'm ready," he said. He flipped a page on the notebook I had given him. "He lives in an apartment building off Sahara Blvd. He doesn't have a dad and runs the streets with some guy named Tony Martin—doesn't sound like our suspect, though. This guy's dark skinned."

"I see. That's not much to go on, but it's a start."

I looked at my watch. "It's getting late. I need to go home and watch my brothers. Let's meet in front of his apartment building tomorrow morning. Maybe we can get a lead on him."

"I'll bring my brother's yearbook. He's a few years ahead of me. Now that we have a name, we can look him up so we know who we're looking for."

"Great idea."

We said goodbye and went our separate ways. I was tired and felt as if we made good headway. I was excited and couldn't wait for tomorrow, but first I needed to check in with Jayden.

I dialed her number while I was walking home. She answered on the first ring. "I've been waiting for you to call. What took you so long?"

"Me? You're the one who hung up on me."

"I didn't have a choice. My mother was yelling at me."

"So, what happened?"

She sighed. I could hear the disappointment in her voice. "Jacob Martindale is not the thief."

"How do you know that?"

"Well, when Jacy got caught, it was Mr. Martindale who did the catching. He called my mom and my mom came over to pick us up."

"How did they catch you?"

"It wasn't hard with the two dogs sitting below the tree I was in, barking at me."

I had a mental picture of Jayden clinging to the tree, two mean dogs barking at her. I laughed. She laughed, too. "I guess it is kind of funny," she said.

"How'd you get down?"

"Mr. Martindale called off his attack dogs and I climbed down. My mother was so angry I thought her head was going to explode. Her face was all red, her lips were sucked inside her mouth and she shook her arm at me so hard I thought it would fall off."

I busted up at the image of my Aunt Jamie with no lips shaking her arm at Jayden. I was sure getting a heavy dose of laughter this evening.

"But what made you realize it wasn't him?"

She sighed again. "His dad told us the reason they moved here was because his company transferred him. I thought for sure it was going to be something really bad, like he killed his wife and was running from the police."

"Really! How do you know he didn't?"

"Because she brought us milk and cookies while Mr. Martindale was giving us a lecture about snooping in places we had no business snooping. Can you believe my mother just sat there letting him yell at us? Poor Jacy…I thought she was going to cry for sure—until the cookies showed up. I've never seen someone recover from a crying fit so quickly." She chuckled. "Anyway, Jacob couldn't have done it because his dad picked him up early from school the day the test was stolen and took him to the dentist."

"Why didn't he just tell you that?"

"I don't know. His dad said he's a math genius. Jacob said he doesn't raise his hand to answer questions because he doesn't want to make the rest of us look bad."

"How nice of him. So where do you stand on your case now that your prime suspect has been eliminated?"

I was pretty sure I could hear her concentrate. "I still have Mark Hesper. He's the guy that someone saw in the hallway after school on the same day the test was stolen."

"I remember him. You were going to check with the football coach to see if he would give him an alibi."

"Right. I had to go to Jacob's house today, so I'm going to go before school starts. My mom said she'd take me early. Jacob even said he'd go with me. It seems he doesn't want a harder test either."

"Okay," I said. "Call me after you talk to the coach."

"Okay, Karrine. Goodnight."

We hung up and I ran the rest of the way home. With the case heating up so much, the last thing I needed was for my mother to ground me.

Chapter Four

I met Jared outside the apartment complex that Stinker Sprinkles lived in. Jared already had his yearbook open and pointed to his picture. The kid was overweight, had bright red hair that stuck straight up, compliments of a bottle of hair gel, and a nose ring in one nostril.

"Yikes," I said. "He won't be hard to miss."

Jared tapped me on the arm and pointed at a kid with bright red hair and baggy pants. He had a nose ring in one nostril. Jared tapped the yearbook. I nodded. We started toward the kid. I tried to play it cool and speak his language. "Yo…Stinker," I said, putting somewhat of a swagger to my walk. "Wassup?"

"What?" Stinker said, wrinkling his nose and squinting. "Who you is, man?"

It killed me, but I said back, "I is Karrine."

"What you want, man?"

Jared said. "We have a few questions for you."

Stinker's eyes flew open wide and I knew Jared had blown it. Stinker turned to run, holding his pants to keep them from falling down. I started running after him. Jared followed. He came to the corner and turned an abrupt right. I skidded to a halt and Jared ran right into me. I lost my balance and stumbled forward. My arms flew about me as I tried to regain it. No such luck, I landed on the pavement with a loud thwack. I cried out in pain "Owwwwww!"

Jared stooped down beside me. "Are you okay?"

I pointed at the fleeing Stinker. Gasping out breaths, I shouted, "Get him."

Jared took off on a run, looking backward he shouted, "Are you going to be okay?"

In answer I got up on my feet and shuffle-ran after them. "Hurry," I yelled.

Jared ran faster, but he just couldn't catch up to him. He stopped, bent over and placed his hands on his knees, panting for breath. I arrived seconds later. "I'm...sor...ry," he panted out.

I sighed. "Aw, it's okay. At least we know we're on the right track."

"What should we do now?"

I glanced at my watch. "Let's hit the bus stop and see if we can get any leads there. We have just enough time before the school bus arrives."

We trotted back the way we came, me doing my shuffle walk, as my ankle was killing me. I was going to have to go to the nurse's office and get some ice when I got to school.

The kids at the bus stop weren't all that cooperative. I decide to dispense with my 'gangsta' jargon and just be myself. I shoved the yearbook under one kid's nose. "What do you know about this guy?"

The kid shoved away the book. He waved a circle around his body. "Dude, you're invadin' my space."

I took one step backward. "Better?"

He nodded and turned up one side of his smile. "It'll do." He took the book from me and grinned. "You mean Stinker. Dude, you just gotta follow your nose."

The kids at the bus stop started laughing. One girl said, "He works after school somewhere, but I don't remember where." She grinned and then looked around to see if everyone was watching her. Then she said, "I only know it's somewhere his smell wouldn't offend people." There was more laughter, and the girl's grin turned boastful.

Another kid asked, "What'd he do?"

"Nothing that I know of," I said. "I just want to question him about a string of car thefts."

"The Mustangs?" another kid asked.

"That's right," I said, closing the yearbook.

Several kids' eyes flew open wide. "He did that?"

"I don't know yet," I said. "It's still too early in my investigation to determine that."

"Dude, you're a detective," the first kid said. He nodded and grinned. "That's cool."

I grinned and puffed out my chest. I handed out a couple business cards. "I'm really looking for a skinny guy he hangs out with. He has brown hair and is just a slight bit taller than I am."

"You got a name?" someone asked.

I sighed. "I'm afraid not."

The girl said, "We'll let you know."

"Thanks," I said.

The school bus came and Jared and I shuffled on with the other kids. The bus was going to the high school, but it would put us closer to our school than walking from here. The bus driver put a hand out to stop us. "I don't recognize you. You got a pass to ride this bus?"

I turned on my charming smile and handed him a business card. "Just let me know if you ever need a mystery solved."

He took the card, examined it, and pocketed it. "I guess one never knows." He let me pass but stopped Jared. "What about you?"

"He's my partner," I said.

The bus driver sighed and let him pass. We heard the doors close and the bus lunged forward, just as we went flying into a vacant seat. The kids laughed at us. I was so pleased I could be their source of morning entertainment.

"I'm pretty sure he did that on purpose," Jared said.

"Yep," I said. "Pretty sure he did."

As the bus bounced along, he picked up several more kids along the way. Jared and I were squished between a guy wearing a green Mohawk and smelling like peppermint, and a guy wearing a bandana and smelling like body odor. We leaned toward Mr. Mohawk.

Jared whispered, "I think we should have walked." I was thinking the same thing.

I couldn't concentrate on the bus, so we got off at the next stop. I turned and waved to the bus driver. "Thanks for the ride," I shouted just as the doors closed and the driver sped off.

"I don't think he liked us much," Jared said.

I got real close to Jared. "Do I smell like body odor?"

He sniffed me and then smiled. "Nope. Do I smell like peppermint?"

I sniffed him back. "Nope."

We started walking in the direction of the school.

"What next?" Jared asked.

I rubbed my chin. I was running out of ideas. Do you realize how hard it is to find a person when you know nothing about him? I didn't think anyone around our school would know who he is since he went to high school and we were only in junior high, but it didn't hurt to ask.

"Let's ask around school," I told Jared. "Perhaps some of the eighth graders might know him."

"I'll ask in gym class," Jared said.

"Good idea."

Finally, the school came into view. I thought we would have to walk forever. We heard the warning bell ring. We had exactly five minutes to make it to our classroom. We looked at each other and took off on a run. I had been late for school three times that month. One more tardy slip and I'd have to spend my afternoon in detention, and I'd most likely be placed on restriction by my mother. Then how would I sleuth?

I slid into my seat in English class just as the tardy bell rang. Mr. Jacobs narrowed his eyes at me. "I was seated when the bell rang," I said.

Mark Jessup said, "She was, Mr. Jacobs."

Mr. Jacobs swung his narrowed eyes Mark's way, turned around, and walked toward the front of the class. "Let's begin with diagramming," he said. I groaned and he sneered. He knew how much I hated diagramming. The rest of the class looked my way, as if it were my fault.

By lunchtime, I was anxious for the school bell to ring. I had come up with some places to look and wanted to get started on it.

Jared slid into the spot next to me. "You find out anything?"

I shook my head. "You?" I asked.

"Yeah. Billy Thornton knows him. He said he hangs with his older brother. He said they belong to some muscle-car club." I raised my eyebrows. Jared grinned. "I know, right."

"What's his name?"

"Billy didn't know. He said he's never actually talked to the guy. He waits on the front porch when he comes over. Then Billy's brother and he go off together."

"Do you think Billy's brother is in on it?"

Jared shrugged. "He didn't say. I didn't want to pry too deeply. I don't know Billy that well and don't know whether he would warn his brother, if he is involved."

I thought about this and nodded. "What about Stinker?"

Jared shook his head. "He didn't know him."

"Hm," I said. "Let's hit Mr. Scoop's place after school. He knows everyone."

We carried our lunch trays to the drop-off spot. Someone bumped me, but when I spun around to say, "Hey," nobody was there. I was just hoisting my tray onto the conveyer belt when I noticed a folded piece of paper lying on it. I took the paper off and dropped my tray onto the belt. "Look at this," I said.

Jared looked over my shoulder. "What is it?"

"A note."

"Where'd it come from?"

"I think the guy who bumped me put it there." I opened it and gasped.

"What!" Jared exclaimed. "What's wrong?"

I handed him the note. He gasped.

I took back the note and read it aloud. "Back off, kid before you get hurt."

I looked around, trying to figure out who had bumped me. Most of the kids had already vacated the cafeteria. The rest of them did not seem in the least bit interested in what Jared and I were doing. I shook my head. "Whoever put this here is gone now."

"Do you think he meant it?"

"I don't know," I said, "but we'd better keep our eyes open."

Jared and I separated. Walking to my Chemistry class, I couldn't help but feel as if a spider were crawling up my back. Everywhere I turned, I swore I heard voices calling my name. Nobody seemed interested in me.

I was relieved when I arrived at the classroom. I took my seat and sighed in relief. My own school had become a place of danger for me.

Halfway through Mr. Edward's lecture, I felt a sudden chill go up my spine. I turned around and saw Andrew Steel staring at me, and his eyes didn't look friendly. I shuddered.

Chapter Five

We went to Mr. Scoop's right after school. I REALLY wanted some strawberry ice cream, and I was sure Mr. Scoops needed some tables wiped down. I was right. The tables were a mess when Jared and I arrived.

"Thank goodness," he said when I walked in the door. "Some women held their monthly book group here and they were here for hours." He swept his hand through the air, indicating the room. "They ate sandwiches and ice cream the entire time. It's surprising those women don't weigh the weight of the shop."

I giggled while I pictured a bunch of women pigging out on ice cream and Mr. Scoops hovering in the background, hoping they would leave. "Never fear," I said, "Karrine is here." I grabbed the dish bucket and began bussing the tables. Jared watched for a moment and then started helping me.

"What brings you in this afternoon?" Mr. Scoops asked. "Aside from the free ice cream." He chuckled.

I stopped wiping and looked at him. Mr. Scoops wasn't getting any younger. I walked up to him and plucked out a gray hair from beneath his cap. "What's this?"

He grabbed his head and let out a yowl. "Why'd you do that?"

I examined the gray hair as if it were a clue. I pointed the hair toward him. "I'm pointing out the obvious." He frowned. I frowned. "Duh, Mr. Scoops, I'm working a case and I need some information."

He rubbed his head where I'd yanked the hair. "Did you have to point out the obvious in such a painful way?"

I grimaced. "Uh, sorry."

He continued to rub his head. I think he was faking. Certainly, it couldn't have hurt that much.

"All right," he said, "tell me about your case."

I settled on a stool. Jared sat next to me. Mr. Scoops handed each of us a strawberry cone. I started licking right away. After my fourth lick, I glanced sideways at Jared. His ice cream was gone and he was licking his fingers. My mouth fell open. "That was fast!" He just grinned.

I was still licking, so he said to Mr. Scoops, "We're looking for a guy named Stinker. Do you know him?"

Mr. Scoops plugged his nose, as if the mere mention of his name created a wafting odor. "Who doesn't know him? You can smell him coming a mile away."

I wrinkled my nose. "Why does he smell so bad?"

Mr. Scoops shrugged. "I heard something about him having stomach problems, but then you know how kids are."

I shook my head. "Yeah. Kids."

"Do you know where he hangs?" Jared asked.

"He works at the Jackson's stables."

I brightened. "I know that place." I had worked a case for Mr. Jackson last year. Someone had painted all his ponies, and I tracked down the perpetrator. It was a tough case, but with the help of Jayden, I cracked it wide open.

We said goodbye and headed off to the stables. Mr. Jackson was pleased to see me, but Mrs. Jackson gave me an evil eye and ran the other way.

"What's wrong with her?" Jared asked.

I didn't really want to talk about it. That was another story and I wanted to concentrate on this one. "She just doesn't like me," I said.

Jared did not ask any more questions about it.

"How's my favorite detective?" Mr. Jackson asked. His smile was so big he could probably shuck an entire cob of corn with only one typewriter ding.

"Hey, Mr. Jackson. I'm on a case," I said.

"Is that right?"

"A really important one."

He winked at me. "My Matilda's not acting up again now, is she?"

"Not that I know of," I said, my huge eyes popping out of my head. How was I supposed to know what his troublemaker wife was up to? "We're looking for someone."

I turned to point at Jared but he wasn't there. "Where'd he go?"

"If you mean your friend, he went that way." Mr. Jackson pointed toward the stable.

Sure enough, he was there and peeking in a window. The window was set high enough to make it difficult to peek in without standing on something, and Jared was standing on a something that didn't look all that safe. Mr. Jackson didn't think so, either.

"Hey! Get off that bucket," he yelled. "What's wrong with that kid," he said. He was running toward the stable. "Didn't your mother teach you any better than that?"

The bucket was wobbling back and forth. Jared was holding on and screaming, "Whoa!" Mr. Jackson arrived just in time. Jared was on his way down when he caught him.

"Thanks, Mister," he said.

Mr. Jackson shook his head at us. "Why would you stand on a paint bucket?"

I jumped in saying, "Jared just wanted to get a better look. We're looking for someone who works here."

"Why didn't you just ask?"

Jared said, "I was looking for the element of surprise. I wanted to catch him in the act."

Mr. Jackson and I both gave Jared a puzzled frown, pulling our eyebrows together. "What act?" he said. I wondered that same question.

"Uh…uh," Jared stuttered, "Gee, I don't know."

I turned toward Mr. Jackson. "Mr. Scoops said Stinker works here part-time. We're looking for him to ask him some questions."

"Did he do something wrong? I should know if one of my employees is a criminal."

"I'm not sure yet," I said. "I need to question him to determine his guilt or innocence."

Several people had come to see Jared's battle with the paint bucket. Lingering in the back of the crowd, I spied him. "There he is!" I exclaimed.

Everyone turned to look as I pointed out Stinker. He saw me pointing at him and took off on a run. "Not again," I said.

I gave chase, into the stables, through a couple of stalls, where horses neighed at our intrusion. I didn't look to see if Jared was behind me. I just assumed he was. Stinker exited the stables and leaped into the riding arena, where several riders were waiting their turn to ride one of the ponies. He grabbed the reins of a beautiful white pony from a little girl. She started crying. Her mother flashed an angry glare and started waving her fist at Stinker. I hated to do it, but I couldn't let Stinker get away. "I need to commandeer a pony," I said. I pointed at Stinker, who was fleeing into the woods. "I can't let my suspect get away."

Someone thrust a set of reins into my hands. "Get him!" a woman shouted. "He has no right to make a girl cry." I couldn't agree more.

I glanced over toward the stable, eager to see if Jared had caught up. He was standing by the stable entrance talking to Cassandra Madigan. She was laughing and curling her hair around her finger. It seemed I had lost my assistant.

My phone rang. I snatched it from my pocket. "Can't talk now," I said. "I'm in pursuit of a suspect."

"Call me back," Jayden said. "It's important."

"I will," I said and shoved the phone back into my pocket.

I didn't even have to give my pony instructions on where to go. He was trained to follow the trail and he didn't let me down. I gave him a little kick in the side and he snorted in anger. Then I remembered Mr. Jackson telling me not to kick the ponies. I clicked my tongue at him and he sped up.

I could see Stinker now. I was about to shout at him when a tree branch hit me in the face. "Ouch!" I yelled. Stinker turned at my shout and laughed at me.

I was just thinking he should watch where he was riding when a large branch knocked him off his pony. He shouted, "Yeow!"

I pulled abruptly on the reins and my pony skidded to a halt. I jumped down and stood over Stinker, hands on hips, wearing my sternest look. "Why do you keep running? I just want to ask you some questions."

"I'll never tell," he said.

"How do you know that unless you let me ask the question?"

"You want to know who my friend is that hangs out with me. You're investigating the Mustang thefts."

My jaw dropped open. Perhaps I should ask him to join my detective agency. It didn't appear Jared was all that interested. Naw, I couldn't stand smelling him all day long. The stable was the perfect place for him. The horses drowned out his stench...well, mostly anyway. "How did you know?"

He shrugged. "Word gets around."

"Well..."

He shrugged again. "I got nothing to say."

The pony he had been riding nudged him in the rear. He fell forward and lost his balance. He ended up on the ground, looking up at me. I put a foot on his chest, anchoring him to the ground. I'd seen this in a cop show once. It usually worked, only I didn't know what to do. So, I just asked him again. "Who's your friend?"

He reached a hand up and flung my foot off his chest. He struggled to his feet (he was easily ten pounds over the recommended weight for a teenager) and stood in front of me. "Look, kid. I don't want to see you get hurt." He looked around, presumably to see if anyone was watching. It made me think twice about being out in the woods with a nearly total stranger—even if he was only a couple years older than I. "This thing here you've involved yourself in is bigger than you think. You need to back off, before you get hurt."

I swallowed a lump in my throat. "Are you threatening me?"

He shook his head and jumped back on his pony. "Just a warning." He trotted off on his pony.

My phone rang again. I looked at caller ID. It was Jayden. I answered quickly. "Sorry, Jayden. I was—"

"Karrine, help me." Her voice was barely a whisper.

"What's wrong?"

"I found out who did it."

"Really! That's great. How'd you do it?"

"Yeah, I know. I went to talk to the football coach. He denied sending Mark after balls. He said if Mark was in the hallway, then perhaps I should be looking at him for the theft."

"Did he do it?"

"No," she whispered.

"Then who did?" I whispered back.

"The coach."

"What!"

"The coach did it," she repeated.

"I heard you. I just couldn't believe it. How'd you find out, and why are we whispering?"

"So he won't hear me."

"Where are you?"

"I'm in the gym. I'm hiding behind the rack of volleyballs."

I still wasn't following. "Tell me what happened."

"I told Mark what the coach said. He was very angry. I followed him to the gym and hid behind the volleyballs. That's how I overheard them talking. Coach told Mark he stole the grade book because Bret Larson is failing math.

If he doesn't pass, he can't play in the tournament, and he's the school's best quarterback. What do I do?"

"March right out there and tell him you've recorded the whole conversation."

"Just like that?"

I hesitated for a moment. What if I gave her bad advice? Could I live with myself if something bad happened? How would I face my Aunt Jamie? Or my grandmother! I heard rustling, the sound of balls bouncing and then Jayden's frenzied, "Ahhhh....."

"What happened?" I screamed.

Jayden didn't come back on the line, but I could hear what was going on.

I heard a man say, "What do you think you're doing?"

Then Jayden said, "I fell and all the balls went bouncing everywhere." Intuition told me to hit record on my phone, and I did.

"I meant, what are you doing here in the gym?"

I heard more rustling on the other end, but I couldn't tell what was going on. It sound like Jayden was standing up.

Suddenly, her voice came through the phone loud and clear. "I know what you did. I recorded your entire conversation with Mark."

"I don't know what you're talking about," the coach said, but I heard wavering in his voice. That usually meant he was squirming, hoping to deny the accusation.

"You stole the grade book so Brett Larson could play in the tournament. Then you tried to blame it on Mark."

"So what," he said. "Just try to prove it."

I heard the sound of loud high heels clicking on the floor. God, I hated being so far away. If only Jayden had Skyped me in. Then I could see what was going on. A soft yet stern voice came through. "Jayden? Why did you leave me a note telling me to come to the gym?"

"It was him," Jayden said.

I could imagine her pointing a finger at him. I didn't know what he looked like, so I just pictured a large man with a big fat belly. Fat because he probably sat around watching football games and eating pretzels all the time. Isn't that what football coaches do?

"He stole your gradebook," Jayden said.

"I did not," he said. "I'll have you expelled for this," he said.

"I can prove it," Jayden said.

I was waiting to find out what happened when a voice came through the phone. It was soft, female, and sounded confused. "Hello?"

"Hello," I said.

"Who is this?"

"My name is Karrine. I run the Crime Solver's Detective Agency. Jayden works for me solving crimes in Sacramento. I'm in Las Vegas."

"Oh," the voice said.

I said, "I think Jayden wanted me to confirm her accusation against the coach. I heard his confession."

"You did?"

"Not only that, but I also recorded it. I'll send the file to Jayden for proof."

"Thank you," she said

Jayden came back on the phone. "Thanks, Karrine. I'll send you a full report tonight."

"Great job, Jayden. I'll talk to you soon. I need to wrap up my own case."

We said goodbye, and I headed back to the stable to see if Jared was done making kissy face with Cassandra Madigan. Cassandra was gone and Jared was helping to feed the horses. He flung his arms into the air when he saw me come trotting up on the pony. "Where have you been? This is no time to be riding ponies. We're here to ask questions."

I lashed out at him. I couldn't help it. My interrogation of Stinker left me in a bad mood. "And how many questions did you ask Cassandra Madigan? Besides 'what is your phone number'. "

He stiffened and narrowed his eyes at me. "Well, as a matter of fact, I asked Cassandra several questions. There's more than one way to get information from a person. Our suspect's name is Cocky Butch."

I relaxed. "I'm sorry. I guess this case is getting to me. Is that his real name?"

"Cassandra didn't know that. She only knows Cocky Butch. She said she's spoken to him on several occasions. Both here when he visits his cousin, and when she does the grocery shopping with her mother on Saturday afternoons. The reason we can't find him is because we're looking in all the wrong places. He's twenty-two. He works at the Stop and Shop. She didn't know what his schedule was, but she sees him at different times. I'm guessing he works varied shifts."

My eyes went wide with surprise, and I don't mind admitting I was a little impressed. It turns out Jared is good at detecting after all. I felt kind of bad for doubting him. "Good job."

"What did you find out?"

I frowned. "Not much I'm afraid. I trapped Stinker after he fell from his pony."

Jared laughed. "He fell off a pony! I wish I had seen that."

I nodded. "Yes, well, he didn't give me much information, but he did warn me to stay away from the case. He said it's bigger than I could imagine." I frowned again as something Jared said poked its way into my brain. "You said he visits his cousin. Who is his cousin?"

Jared grinned. "Stinker."

My mouth fell open. "That little rat," I said. "Of course he won't give us information. He's protecting his cousin."

"And maybe himself, too," Jared added. "He just might be involved."

I nodded. "I had thought of that. Why else would he keep running from us?"

"Let's sleep on this and pick up where we left off tomorrow. It's getting late and my brain is tired."

Jared agreed and we went our separate ways. I thought about it all through dinner, reading my brothers a bedtime story, and as I readied myself for bed. Something in the back of my mind was nagging me, and I couldn't figure out what it was. Perhaps a good night sleep might help.

Chapter Six

I woke the next morning just knowing I'd break open the case. I got up extra early, made my way downstairs, where I smelled delicious pancakes cooking. Yummy. I was more than ready for some nourishment. I downed three big ones and ate the egg Mother insisted I eat. Apparently pancakes don't have any nutritional value, Mother's words, not mine. I fail to see how anything so delicious could not have something valuable to add.

I brushed my teeth and ran for the door. "I'll be late today," I yelled. I slammed the door before Mother could object.

I met Jared at the Shop and Save, where we intended to hold a stakeout until it was time to go to school. We hunkered down near some bushes next to the store.

"Is it necessary to get up this early?" Jared whined. "I normally wouldn't rise for another half hour."

I grinned at him. "I guess you didn't have your pancakes and eggs." I flexed my muscles. "I'm alert and ready to go."

Jared stared at me. One eye nearly closed and, in a mimicry voice, said, "No, I didn't have pancakes and eggs. I didn't have time for pancakes and eggs."

I reached into my backpack and pulled out a protein bar. I kept them in my backpack in case I ever got stuck on a stakeout and couldn't make it home for dinner. I handed it to him. "Here, this will help."

He stared at it for a moment, hunched his shoulders, mumbled something I couldn't understand, and snatched the bar from my hands. He ripped off the wrapper and chewed without enthusiasm. I shook my head, "Whatever."

Jared glowered at me, then hit me in the arm and pointed his finger at the Shop and Save. "I think that's him."

I turned to look, saw a tall guy with brown hair, the exact description the pizza guy had given us. "He's the right age, right height, and right hair color." A moment later, Stinker came around a corner and started talking to him. "It's got to be him."

I pulled out a pair of binoculars and got a closer look.

"Hey!" Jared said. "I want some of those."

"Sorry, only one pair," I said, just as Jared grabbed them from my hands. "Hey!" I yelled.

"I'll give them right back."

I sighed and let him have them. "Can you tell what they're saying?"

"No," Jared said. "I don't read lips."

I grabbed back the binoculars. "I do," I said, smiling smugly.

Jared gave an exaggerated sigh. "What are they saying then, smarty pants?"

"Something about a meeting after school, and the boss wants to step up something. It's kind of hard because I'm only getting one side of the conversation. Stinker has his back to me." Stinker turned sideways then. I gasped.

"What?" Jared asked.

"He's talking about me."

"What's he saying?"

I paled and sat down hard. "He said I'm in the way and they have to get rid of me."

"This is bad, Karrine. Maybe your mother was right. Perhaps this is too big for us."

I swallowed hard and nodded. I bit back tears I did not want to come. "Let's just go to school."

I thought about our situation all through school. In English class I got lost in the world of complex diagramming and was able to take my mind off the case. But in History class, nothing could attract my mind to the boring old Civil War. I traced back the case to the beginning. What would two barely grown men want with old Mustangs?

Until today, I hadn't realized just how dangerous this case was. Perhaps it would be best to let it drop, but could I? Could I walk away from the biggest case of my career? Of course, I could. It wasn't just my life in danger here. Jared was in danger, too.

When the bell rang, I ran to meet Jared. Mr. Singleton, the janitor, was already busy in the hallway mopping the floor. He was whistling a tune and swishing his mop back and forth.

I waited impatiently, checking my watch every few moments for any signs of Jared. Where could he be? We had agreed to meet by the front door. Maybe he got in trouble in class and had to stay behind. That was it. I knew he had P.E last period, so I headed for the gym.

When I passed Mr. Singleton, he stopped mopping and said hello. I gave a little wave and continued on my way.

Most of the kids had already gone. Kids these days don't waste any time getting out of the school. One minute extra in the classroom might cause us to use up all our brain cells at once. We had to save some for high school.

I took out my cell phone to call my mother. I wanted to remind her I'd be late, so she wouldn't worry. I got her voicemail and left a message. I told her I'd home in an hour, and if she wouldn't mind making some, I'd love some chocolate chip cookies. Hers were the best.

Kenny Persimmons passed me. "Hey, Karrine."

"Hey, Kenny." Then I remembered he and Jared had P.E. class together. "Is Jared still in the gym?" I asked.

Kenny shook his head. "Nope. He wasn't in class today."

"Sure he was," I said. "I saw him right before class started. We agreed to meet near the front doors of the school. I've been waiting for a half hour. He hasn't shown up."

"I'm telling ya he wasn't in class. Maybe he got sick and went home."

I frowned. "Maybe," I said, but I didn't convince myself.

Kenny started to walk away, but I wasn't done yet. "How sure are you?"

"Look, Karrine. I'm not blind and I know Jared wasn't in class. I have to go now and be tortured by the orthodontist. I'll see you later."

He ran past me. I heard the sound of running feet, sneakers slide on the highly waxed floor, and then the glass on the doors at the front of the school. I turned away from the gym and went back to the office. If I were lucky, maybe the nurse would still be there and she could tell me if Jared had gone home sick.

Mr. Singleton was gone, having finished the floor. I saw his cart in the hallway and figured he was cleaning up the trash all the kids left behind when they went home.

She was just locking the door when I arrived, winded from hurrying through the hallway. "Ms. Abraham!" I called, waving my arms frantically.

"Heavens, Child," she said. She put a hand on my shoulder to steady me. "Is the building on fire or something?"

I shook my head. "I can't find Jared."

She looked at me with those eyes that grownups get when kids displease them. "Is running down the hallway going to help you find Jared? Mr. Singleton just mopped these floors. What if you slipped on them? You'd probably break an arm." She got a frightened look on her face. "Oh, dear—or worse—you could crack open your head—or maybe even break your back. Then the ambulance would have to come and take you away." Her eyes got wide. "What would I say to your mother?" She looked into my eyes. "She'd probably sue the school."

I put my hand on her arm to stop her talking—before she had me lying dead on the floor. "It's okay, Ms. Abraham. I promise not to run anymore."

She relaxed and a slight smile came to her lips. "Thank you, dear, and for heaven's sake, child, go home. It's well past the time school ended."

I sighed. "You're sure you haven't seen Jared. He didn't show up for last class. I thought maybe he got sick and went home."

"Positive. Now, I have to go. Mr. Abraham is taking me out to the movies. It's my birthday."

She said this with pride, as if having a birthday was a big accomplishment for her. I guess when you get that old, every birthday is a cause to celebrate. I waved "Have fun," I said.

She finished locking her door and made her way to the front door. Her skirt swished and her shoes made a lot of noise as she walked. I think the excitement over her birthday made her look just a little bit younger.

Mr. Singleton was back and was mopping again. He grinned when I walked by and raised his hand to wave again. I brought my eyebrows together and slowly waved. Just how clean did he think the hallway needed to be?

The gym was at the very end of the main hallway. I stood in front of the gym doors. I had a decision to make. Should I knock on the door or just walk in? Chances were pretty good that all the boys had gone home. I looked both ways down the hallway. The only thing I saw was Mr. Singleton whistling and mopping. He turned around, stared at me for a minute, and waved again. I waved and when he turned back around, I went inside.

Chapter Seven

The gym was cold and dark. A chill ran down my spine. Suddenly, I was glad Mr. Singleton was only a shout away. "Jared," I softly called. He did not answer. Then a little more loudly I said, "Jared, are you in here?" I heard a noise and jumped. "Jared," I said. "You were supposed to meet near the front doors."

I looked at my watch. I should be headed for home by now. If I didn't hurry, Mother was going to worry. I heard the noise again and took out my phone. Maybe I should call her and let her know what was going on. I let it ring five times and when she didn't answer I hung up and sent her a text. Suddenly, a thought struck me. What if I got it wrong? Then I started to doubt myself. What if we had planned to meet at Mr. Scoop's place instead? Everybody knows I do my best thinking over ice cream. I dialed his number.

"Mr. Scoops speaking. How may I help you today? Tutti-Frutti, bubblegum, chocolate…all of the above?" He chuckled.

His laughter put me at ease. I laughed, too. "Hey, Mr. Scoops. It's me, Karrine."

"Hey there. How's the master detective today?"

"Not very well," I said. "I can't find Jared. I thought we were supposed to meet at the entrance of the school, but he's not here and Kenny said he wasn't in P.E last period."

"And you want to know if he's here."

"Yeah," I said. "I'm wondering if I forgot where we were supposed to meet. Is he there?"

"I'm afraid not," he said. "Too bad, too. I could sure use the help."

I sighed. "Okay. If he comes in will you call me?"

"Sure thing, kiddo."

I hung up the phone and turned to walk back out of the gym. It certainly didn't look like Jared was there. I pulled open the door and heard the noise again. Then

Jared came running and knocked right into me. "What! Jared, where have you been, we were suppo—"

"Run, Karrine." Jared pushed me through the door and kept pushing me down the hallway.

When I stopped, winded from my run, I panted out, "What—is—going—on?" I didn't know what we were running from, but I wasn't about to stick around to find out.

"It's Stinker," Jared shouted. He was pulling me along now, his hand gripping my hand in a tight grip.

"Stinker's here?"

Then he was in front of us, and I had no idea how that happened. We stopped running, panting as we stood staring at Stinker. He was only about twenty steps from us. "This way," Jared shouted.

We ran toward the cafeteria. Maybe Mr. Singleton had moved on to there. He could help us. We burst through the doors as if we were making a grand entrance. There was no sign of Mr. Singleton. Jared pulled me into the kitchen. We crouched down beside the stove. There must be a whole bunch of kids eating hot lunch because that stove was huge.

We couldn't see a thing from our hiding place, but we could hear, and when the doors to the cafeteria opened, my heart stopped beating…well, not really, but it sure felt like it. I had worked in the cafeteria before and I knew there was a back door that was kept locked. I waved my hand and urged Jared toward the door.

What I didn't know was that it had an alarm on it. When Jared twisted the lock and pushed open the door, a shrill noise sounded so loudly that it hurt my eardrums. We both put our hands over our ears and ran for it.

"The front doors," I said.

"We should just hide," Jared said. "Surely that alarm will bring help from the police."

I shouted back. "I don't think the alarm goes to the police—just in here." We could, of course do what Jared said and hide until help arrived. Mr. Singleton must be able to hear the alarm where he was.

We could see the door come into view. "There," I said, pointing at the door.

"Stop right there," Stinker yelled at us.

"Hurry, Karrine," Jared said.

Stinker was gaining on us. He was just enough older than us that he could run faster. I had an inspiration. Yesterday, my mother had asked me to buy her mayonnaise on the way home. She liked the kind in the squirt bottle. I had forgotten to give it to her. It was still in my backpack. Still running, I shifted the backpack to my front and opened the zipper. I found the mayonnaise and tore open the seal. Stinker was so close now I could smell him. Reaching down, I squeezed as hard as I could. Mayonnaise squirted all over Mr. Singleton's clean floor. I winced when I heard Stinker yell. He had hit the mayonnaise right on and was going down.

Jared started laughing. "That was brilliant, Karrine."

I grinned with pride. "Yes, but he's not going to stay down long. Hurry up and get to the front doors."

We ran as fast as we could. I chanced a glance back and saw that Stinker was still down. I think his ankle was either sprained or broken because he was holding it tightly against him. I felt kind of bad for about two seconds. Then I remembered the look on Mrs. Thornton's face when I promised to find the people who stole her Mustang.

We were almost to the door when a man stepped through the door, blocking our way. I felt momentary relief until I saw who it was. Cocky Butch stood just inside the door, his legs spread apart, arms folded across his chest, and he was laughing. He wore black pants, black shirt, black vest, and a collar around his neck with spikes on it! "Yikes."

We skidded to a halt. Jared slipped but got right back up. What were we to do? We were trapped. I glanced back at Stinker. Maybe we could just retreat the way we had come. That wasn't going to happen. Stinker was on his feet, limping, so obviously it was just a sprain. He sure was angry, though. If he were one of those comic strips, steam would be coming from his head.

"What are we going to do?" Jared asked.

It was time to stop panicking and put on my detective cap. There was a possibility that Ms. Sweet, the secretary was in her office, but we'd have to get past Cocky Butch, and it was only a chance—not worth taking.

Stinker was getting closer. If I didn't make a decision now Stinker would cut off access to the other hallways. "Mr. Singleton!" I shouted. "He's still here."

"That's right," Jared said.

We only had to make it back about fifty feet. We turned. "Go!" Jared shouted.

We ran as fast as we could, taking the turn around the corner so fast that we nearly collided with the wall. Stinker couldn't go any faster with his sprained ankle, but Cocky Butch had full use of his legs.

"Faster!" I shouted.

"I'm going as fast as I can."

I was a good runner, so I grabbed Jared's hand and pulled him up to my speed.

"I have an idea."

"What?" Jared asked.

I still had my backpack on as a front pack. I took out my history book and threw it at Cocky Butch. Then I grabbed my English book and did the same thing. Jared caught on and started doing the same thing. His Geography book hit Cocky Butch square in the middle of his forehead. My plan was to knock him off his feet, just as we had done with Stinker. Since neither of them went to this school, they probably didn't know the way to the janitor's closet. If we could slow them down, we could get there in time. I was reaching for another book when my hand bumped a bag of something. I grabbed whatever it was and pulled it out. "Yes!" I shouted. I held in my hand my little brother's bag of marbles. He must have put them there when we went to our grandmother's house.

Jared glanced over and grinned. "Oh, please let me!"

I grinned back. "We share."

I took half the bag of marbles, which was difficult to do while running, and passed the rest of the bag to Jared. "Count of three," I said. "One, two, three!" We let the marbles go and saw both Stinker and Cocky Butch try to avoid them. Stinker, his one leg already injured, went down in a hurry. Screaming curse words at us. I was afraid it wasn't going to work when all of a sudden Cocky Butch was on the ground.

"Yes!" Jared and I both exclaimed.

We only had two more corners to hit and we were there.

We made it in time. We were about to push open the door when I noticed the nameplate on it. They'd be able to find us by it. Jared must have read my mind because he reached up and ripped it from the door. He pushed open the door and we fell, tumbling and out of breath, on the other side.

"Mr….Singleton…help," I panted out.

He was in his chair at his desk, writing something down. He turned and looked us, not seeming to be at all surprised to see us.

"What's the matter, kids?" he asked. He grinned and the grin didn't look much like *an, I want to help you grin.*

Jared had recovered his breath and said, "We figured out who stole the Mustangs."

"And now… they're…after us," I panted out.

Mr. Singleton rose and suddenly he didn't look at all like the little old janitor nobody ever paid attention to. He seemed taller now, and more confident, too—as if he were in charge.

The door opened. In limped Cocky Butch and Stinker.

"There they are!" Jared shouted, but I was watching Mr. Singleton, and the pieces were beginning to fall into place.

I whispered, "It was you, Mr. Singleton."

Cocky Butch said, "What should we do with them, Boss?"

Jared looked confused. "I don't under…." But then he did. "Oh, no!"

Oh, no, was right. I had led us straight into the pit. My detective radar must be on the fritz. Surely I should have noticed the odd way in which Mr. Singleton kept mopping the same floor. He was keeping watch of what I was doing.

"Why?" I asked. "You have a good job."

"Ha!" he shouted. Anger flushed his face red. "A good job, you say. Nobody appreciates what I do. I clean up all day long after you brats. Spilled milk on the cafeteria tables? No worries, Mr. Singleton will clean it up. Spit balls all over the classrooms…and I have no idea why the teachers don't put a stop to it. Oh wait, I know. 'It's okay, Mr. Singleton will clean them up.' And the worst of it is the wads of gum I have to scrape from under the desks. Nobody cares what I think. Nobody cares how hard I work."

"But it's your job," Jared protested. "They pay you to do it."

Mr. Singleton rushed forward, his hand curled into a fist, which he shook at Jared. Jared pulled himself back, fearing Mr. Singleton was about to punch him, but he didn't. He said, "You think this job pays enough to clean up after you brats. It barely pays the bills. Tie them up in the corner," he said.

Cocky Butch stepped forward and grabbed my arm. Stinker grabbed Jared. They both pushed us toward the corner.

I wasn't about to give up that easily. "Do you really think kidnapping two kids is worth the money you get selling those stolen Mustangs?"

He laughed. "Little girl, you have no idea how much vintage Mustangs are worth. One of those cars brings in more money than I make in six months."

"But kidnapping is a serious crime. You'll go to prison."

Mr. Singleton laughed again, "Only if they catch me. I have one more job to do and then I'm heading out of the country. By the time anyone finds you, I'll be on my way to Mexico."

I struggled against my ropes. "You'll never get away with this."

They finished tying us up and walked to the office door. There was a bunch of noise on the other side. The door flew open and in came Mr. Scoops. He wore his apron all stained with various flavors of ice cream, and his funny paper hat. His right hand held his ice cream scoop. "Karrine!"

"Watch out, Mr. Scoops."

Mr. Scoops turned to look just as Cocky Butch threw a net over him. "What?" he said. "What is going on here?"

"Can't anyone mind their own business?" Mr. Singleton asked.

My mother came through the door next. She wore her kitchen apron and waved her rolling pin in the air. It seemed everyone was getting my message at once.

"Okay, Karrine. What are you doing here? You are late coming home. I have two pies in the oven and you're not answering your phone. I had to ask Mrs. Thornton to look after your brothers. Why aren't you answering your phone?"

"Who is this lady," Mr. Singleton asked.

"Who am I?" My mother asked. "Who are you?" She wore a threatening look on her face and continually ranted on, as if there weren't three car thieves in the room, and two kids tied up in chairs, not to mention the ice cream man lying on the floor with a big net over him.

Mother looked at me, then at Mr. Singleton. "What is going on here?"

Mr. Singleton nodded in my mother's direction, looking at Cocky Butch. "Tie her up with the rest."

Cocky Butch grabbed one arm and Stinker grabbed the other.

"Now just a minute," my mother said. Then she took a deep breath. "Oh good Lord, what is that smell?" She turned accusing eyes toward Stinker. "Say 'excuse me,' young man. Didn't your mother teach you any manners?"

"You might want to be quiet, Mom."

"I'm not going to let this man push me around." She shook her rolling pin at him. "If you keep this nonsense up, I'll bop you over the head with my rolling pin."

Cocky Butch came up behind her and grabbed both her arms. Stinker got duct tape and wrapped her arms together. Then they sat her in a chair next to me and tied her to it.

"Now look her—"

Mr. Singleton put tape across her mouth. I groaned. I *had* warned her.

The three of them walked out the door. I heard it lock. Immediately I started trying to get out of my binds. They were tight, but it was after all Stinker who tied me—Stinker, who probably flunked three grades by now.

I rocked my chair until I was back to back with Jared. I wriggled my fingers and managed to get hold of Jared's knot. Working carefully, I managed to untie the knot. Jared jumped up out of the chair and waved his hands in the air, singing, "I'm free…I'm free."

"Ah, a little bit of help here," I said.

"Oh, right." Jared untied my hands. Then I untied my mother. All three of us worked on freeing Mr. Scoops. So much for us being rescued.

"What now?" Jared asked.

"Come on," I said, running toward the door. "I think I know where they're going."

"Just a minute, young lady," my mother said.

"But Mom, they're going to get away. Mr. Singleton said they're going to Mexico. We have to stop them. I promised Mrs. Thornton."

Mother grinned. "I just want you to wait for me." She giggled. "This is kind of fun."

We all ran out the door. Mr. Scoops asked, "Where are we going?"

"There's only one other family I know of that has a Mustang that old, older even than the rest. And fully restored. It's worth a bundle of money."

Jared's mouth fell open. "I didn't know you knew so much about cars."

"I don't really," I said, "but remember the day we went to the Pizza House and you were so concerned about getting the extra thin pizza because of the carbs?"

Jared turned red when Mr. Scoops laughed at him.

"What about it?" Jared asked between clenched teeth.

"I talked to Jimmy. He knows all about cars. He said there were only a few old Mustangs around. He said the Greene's have the most expensive Mustang around. That has to be where they're going to hit next."

We piled into Mom's minivan. I dialed the police on the way and told them what was going on. The sergeant was reluctant to take me seriously until Mr. Scoops got on the phone and told them I knew what I was talking about.

"Do we even know where the Greenes live?" Mother asked. "I have no clue where I'm going."

"They live on Oakland Park Road." Jared said. "I used to deliver papers to them."

"That's off Sahara Blvd," I told Mom.

"I know where that is," she said. She stepped hard on the accelerator. I didn't know Mother knew how to drive that fast.

The police weren't there when we arrived. We sat in the van, watching the house. Night was just beginning to descend, but there was still plenty of light.

"There they are," I said, pointing to the house.

Mr. Singleton and Cocky Butch were just rounding the house on the way to the back yard. They looked around, checking to see if anyone was watching. We were, but they didn't know that.

I opened the car door and started to get out. Mother grabbed my arm to stop me. "Oh, no, you don't."

I opened wide as I saw a gun coming through the window and pointing directly at Mother. The hand that held the gun belonged to Stinker. "Get out," he said. We all got out. "Move," he said, nodding in the direction of the garage. "In there."

We slowly made our way to the garage. None of us dared make a move, as Stinker still had the gun pointed at Mother. "All right," she said when he nudged her in the ribs with it. "I'm moving."

"Open it," Stinker said.

I opened the side door and stepped inside. Cocky Butch and Mr. Singleton looked in our direction.

"What the…" Mr. Singleton said.

"Look who followed us."

"What is wrong with you people?" Mr. Singleton said. "I've tried to be nice about this, but you're not leaving me any other choice." He took the gun from Stinker and motioned for us to move. "Up against the wall," he said.

Before we could move, we heard sirens screaming outside. Mr. Singleton turned his head away and Mr. Scoops rushed him, knocking the gun from his hand. I jumped on Stinker's back, gagging and nearly puking from the smell. Jared knocked into Cocky Butch and Mother sat on him.

Mr. Scoops got the gun and pointed it at Mr. Singleton. Stinker started laughing. "It ain't loaded."

The door going into the house opened and police officers rushed in, taking the three men into custody. The sergeant in charge approached us. He looked at my mother. "I take it you're Karrine."

I stepped forward. "I am."

He looked at me with a shocked expression. Then he grinned. "Not bad, kid. We've been trying to break open this ring for a long time."

I grinned and saluted him. "Crime Solver's Detective Agency at your service, Sir."

He chuckled and walked back into the house.

"Let's go home now," Mother said.

"I have a better idea," Mr. Scoops said. "Let's celebrate with a party. Free ice cream for everyone."

We all cheered as we piled back into the van. When we got to the ice cream parlor everyone went inside. "I have to make a phone call," I said. "I'll be there in a minute."

Jayden answered the phone on the second ring. "Crime Solver's Detective Agency, Jayden speaking. How may I solve a crime for you?"

I laughed. "It's me, Karrine. I solved the crime."

"All right!" she said. "Tell me all about it."

I told her the story and she cheered. "I have to go now," I said, "but I'll see you on summer break."

"I can't wait," Jayden said. "I hope we have a really big crime to solve."

"See you soon."

We hung up and I joined the others for ice cream, smiling at the thought that I finally solved my first big case.

As I sat down, Mother waved her spoon at me and said to me, "By the way, you're grounded for a week."

"For what?" I asked.

"Disobeying me and working the case."

I started to object the accusation, but instead I just sighed. Everyone at the table laughed, except me. I just shook my head. Does any other detective get grounded by her mother? Jeez!

www.ingramcontent.com/pod-product-compliance
Lightning Source LLC
Chambersburg PA
CBHW071326130626
46556CB00004B/1763